W9-BYA-632

Aurora's Sleepy Kitten

For Marissa and Gabby —T.R.

Published in the United States by Random House Children's Books, a division of Random House LLC, 1745 Broadway, New York, NY 10019, and in Canada by Random House of Canada Limited, Toronto, Penguin Random House Companies, in conjunction with Disney Enterprises, Inc. Random House and the colophon are registered trademarks of Random House LLC.

randomhousekids.com

Educators and librarians, for a variety of teaching tools, visit us at RHTeachersLibrarians.com

ISBN 978-0-7364-3266-5 (trade)
ISBN 978-0-7364-8163-2 (lib. bdg.)

Printed in the United States of America
10 9 8 7 6 5 4 3 2 1

Random House Children's Books supports the First Amendment and celebrates the right to read.

By Tennant Redbank

Illustrated by the Disney Storybook Art Team

Random House New York

"Beauty! Beauty, wake up!"

Beauty's little pink nose wiggled. Her ears twitched. She opened one eye.

First she saw grass. Then she saw flowers. Then she saw Princess Aurora. She was kneeling next to Beauty in the garden!

Aurora ruffled the fur around Beauty's collar.

"Sorry to wake you, but the royal star-gazers just told me the most wonderful news!" the princess said. "They've been watching the skies, and so have the three good fairies. They all agreed. Tonight there will be a star shower!"

A star shower? Beauty sat up. She had never seen a star shower. It sounded so unusual!

Aurora clasped her hands together. "A star shower is the most beautiful thing in the world. Hundreds of stars tumble down through the night sky. It's like a waterfall of stars."

Oooh, that *did* sound beautiful. Beauty couldn't wait to see it!

"Will you watch it with me?" Aurora asked. The good fairies hoped Beauty would join, too.

Beauty meowed. Of course she would! She loved Aurora. She would do anything for the princess. Nothing would stop her from—

"It's at midnight," Aurora added.

Midnight?

Beauty's whiskers drooped.

Uh-oh.

Midnight was not good. Beauty had

never stayed awake until midnight. She hardly ever stayed up past eight o'clock!

Every time she tried, she thought of how lovely it felt to snooze. Then—*zzzz*. She fell asleep.

How would she make it to midnight?

Aurora gave Beauty a kiss and a quick cuddle.

"I'm glad you'll be there," the princess said. "But I have so much to do! I'm planning a party for the star shower!" Then she danced away from Beauty and across the garden.

Normally, Aurora didn't care that

Beauty was so sleepy. But Beauty had a feeling Aurora would be sad if her pet kitten slept through the star shower. And the party!

Beauty put her head on her paws. She and Aurora were so much alike. They both liked pretty things. They both liked yummy treats. Most of all, they both liked napping. In fact, that was how Beauty had first met the princess.

Beauty thought about that day and sighed.

She had fallen asleep while playing with her kitten friends. She didn't know

she was in the palace garden. Three good fairies found her there. They had wanted to wake her, but Aurora asked them to let her sleep. When Beauty did wake up, she was Aurora's pet from then on.

Even though Beauty and Aurora were a lot alike, there was one big difference. When she wanted to, Aurora could stay awake.

But Beauty? Not in a million years.

"What am I going to do?" Beauty asked herself.

Beauty needed help. She knew just whom to ask—Bloom.

Bloom was Beauty's pony and friend. She had a pretty purple mane and tail. But more importantly, Bloom was very smart.

Beauty looked all over for the purple pony. She finally found her in the courtyard. Bloom was watching three workers.

They were setting up a stage for a puppet show.

"There you are!" Beauty said. She sat down next to Bloom on the cobblestones. The sun had made them nice and warm.

"Hi, Beauty," Bloom said. "How's everything?"

"Aurora wants me to go to the star shower tonight," Beauty said.

"That's great!" Bloom said.

"It's at midnight," Beauty added.

"Oh," Bloom said. "Not so great." She knew all about how sleepy Beauty was. "How will you ever stay up?"

"I have no idea," Beauty said. She put her head down and closed her eyes. She had to think. The warm cobblestones were nice. She felt so—

Beauty shook herself awake.

She had almost fallen asleep again!

"It's no use," Beauty said. "I'll never be able to make it to midnight."

Bloom tossed her mane. "Maybe you've got it backward," she said. "Maybe you don't need to stay awake. Maybe you need to sleep."

"Sleep?" Beauty asked. What did Bloom mean?

"Yes!" Bloom said. "Sleep now. Sleep all day. Then tonight you'll be rested. You won't be able to sleep!"

Beauty purred. What a lovely idea!

"You're so smart," she told Bloom. "Sleeping is my favorite thing to do. I'm very good at it! In fact, I'll sleep right

here." She laid her head back down on the sun-warmed stones. She closed her eyes.

BANG! BANG! BANG!

Beauty's eyes snapped open.

"Maybe this isn't the best spot," Bloom said. She nodded toward the puppet stage. The workers were hammering nails into the side of it.

"That's okay," Beauty said. "I'll nap in my own bed."

She said goodbye to Bloom and went to her room. Her bed was in the corner.

Beauty padded over to it. It was well

used. She spent hours in it every day and night! But one of the seams had split. A clump of stuffing stuck out of the side, and she nosed it back into place. Then she tried to even out the lumps. She lay down and closed her eyes. Ah, peace and—

Swish, swish, swish. Splash! Slop.

Quiet? Hardly!

A cleaning crew was working in the hall. After a few minutes, they moved into Beauty's room. They dusted. They swept. They washed and mopped and scrubbed. It was so noisy!

Beauty spotted her golden tiara nearby.

She slipped it on. Then she left the room. She stepped around the puddles and bubbles on the floor.

"I'll just find another place," she said.

She tried the garden. People were setting up chairs and tables.

Rattle, rattle, clatter.

She tried the tower. The good fairies were making magic firecrackers for the party. Merryweather tested one.

KerPOW!

No chance Beauty could sleep there!

Finally, Beauty went to the stables. The stables were usually quiet. She found an empty stall and settled in. But she still heard banging and scraping. She heard hammering and sawing.

Preparing for parties was very noisy!

Then Beauty heard tapping, too. It sounded like dancing. . . .

Beauty peeked her head out.

It was Bloom!

"Oh, hi, Beauty," Bloom said. "I thought you were taking a nap in your bedroom."

Beauty sighed. "It's no use," she said. "I can't sleep. Everyone is getting ready for the party and making so much noise."

"I know what you mean," Bloom said. "I want to dance a special dance tonight for Aurora—a star dance! But it's too busy around here to practice."

Bloom leaned closer to Beauty. "Hey, I know a place where it's quiet."

"Where?" Beauty asked.

"The woods!" Bloom said.

"The woods?" Beauty gulped. She had never been in the woods before.

Beauty was a palace kitten. She was used to a pampered life. She had a dozen ribbons and bows. She was wearing her own tiara. Aurora fed her caviar.

So what if her bed was a little lumpy? She was hardly roughing it.

Beauty had heard about the woods.

Wild animals lived there. It was dark. There were pricker bushes and burrs that got stuck in a kitten's fur.

But the woods didn't have parties. It was quiet.

And Beauty had to get some sleep. She would do anything for Aurora . . . even go into the woods.

"Sure," she told Bloom, but her voice wavered. She wasn't sure at all.

Bloom pranced ahead. "Follow me," she said. "I know a great spot for sleeping!"

Bloom led Beauty out the palace gate. They took the road to the edge of the woods. A dirt path wove between the trees.

"There's nothing to be scared of," Beauty said to herself. She stepped onto the path and entered the trees.

As she walked, she relaxed. She expected the woods to be spooky, but they were really quite nice. They weren't dark. They just weren't very bright. And that was perfect for sleeping.

Thick grass filled the paths. They muffled Bloom's hoofbeats. That was good for sleeping, too.

"Here we are!" Bloom said, dashing

ahead. The path turned and Bloom turned with it—and vanished.

"Bloom?" Beauty called. She followed the path. She peeked around the corner.

Whoa!

Bloom was standing in the middle of a circle of trees. Dark green ferns poked up from the dirt. Moss covered the ground. The clearing was quiet and peaceful.

Now, *this* was a perfect spot for a nap!

"What do you think?" Bloom asked.

"It's wonderful!" Beauty said. She lay down on the velvety moss. It was even softer than her bed.

Bloom started to dance. Her hooves tapped the ground.

"Does my dancing bother you?" she asked Beauty.

"No," Beauty said with a yawn. "It's nice."

She thought about staying awake to watch Bloom's star dance. But she knew she'd rather sleep.

Beauty's eyes drooped shut and she drifted off.

Suddenly, a loud hooting noise came from outside the pine circle. Beauty sat up. Bloom stopped dancing.

"Wh-what was that?" Bloom asked.

Beauty gulped. "I don't know," she said. She moved closer to Bloom. The sound was creepy. It was haunting. A dark shadow swept over them.

Maybe it was a ghost!

Beauty and Bloom heard a *whoosh*. Above them, leaves trembled.

"It's coming this way!" Bloom cried. She buried her head under her fluffy tail and squeezed her eyes shut.

Beauty's fur was standing on end. All thoughts of sleep were gone. But she didn't hide. She didn't shut her eyes. She had to protect her friend from the ghost!

"Grrr," Beauty growled, like a little pink tiger. She swiped at the air with her paw.

The hooting sound came again. It was closer now. . . .

With a flap of its wings, a brown owl swept into the circle of trees.

Beauty let out her breath.

Bloom's head was still hidden under her tail.

"You can look now," Beauty whispered to her. "It's an owl!"

"An owl?" Bloom said. She poked her head out. "Oh, sure," she said. "That makes sense, with the hooting and all. We just don't have any owls at the palace. That's why I didn't know."

Beauty smiled. She had been so scared to come into the woods. But in a pinch, she had been brave for her friend. Maybe she was more than just a pampered kitten.

The owl flew over to Beauty and Bloom. "I haven't seen you here before," he said. "*Whooo* are you? What brings you to the woods?"

"I'm Beauty," Beauty said. "And this is Bloom. We're Princess Aurora's pets."

As she spoke, other critters came out

of the woods. Little yellow, blue, and pink birds flew over from high branches. Squirrels scrambled down the trees. Chipmunks popped out of holes in the ground. Bunnies hopped across the forest floor. They all seemed interested in what Beauty was saying.

"Aurora?" one of the bunnies said. "That's Briar Rose! We knew her ages ago. Back then, she didn't know she was a princess!"

"She didn't?" Beauty asked.

"Nope," a squirrel answered. "She lived in a quiet little cottage with her three

aunts. Of course, they weren't her real aunts. They were three good fairies."

"They were? She did?" Beauty echoed.

She had never heard about this part of Aurora's life. She had no idea Aurora had so many forest friends!

Bloom got to her hooves. "A quiet cottage?" she repeated. "Beauty, don't you see? That's perfect for us!"

Beauty nodded. "You're right!" she said. She explained to the owl and squirrels, birds, chipmunks, and bunnies about the star shower. And about the party. And about midnight. And about how terribly sleepy she was. The animals were very understanding.

"We'll take you to the cottage," a yellow bird twittered.

"You'll get plenty of rest there," added a blue bird.

"Come on!" called a pink bird, who led the way.

The animals passed birches and oaks. They passed fallen logs. They passed spots where the trees were so thick, the owl decided to say farewell. They crossed a gully. Finally, they saw the cottage ahead of them.

The cottage was nestled into the roots of a grand old tree. It had a thatched roof and a brick chimney. Next to it, a stream turned a waterwheel.

Bloom pushed open the door. Directly across the floor was a set of stairs.

"This way," a bunny said. He hopped ahead of Beauty up the staircase.

Beauty followed him a little more slowly. The cottage looked so interesting! She wouldn't mind having a peek around first.

Then she shook her head. That would be silly. Sleeping was better than anything, right? It was even better than looking around Aurora's old home.

At the top of the stairs was a room with a cozy bed. Beauty leaped onto it.

"This was Briar Rose's bed," the bunny said.

"I can tell," Beauty said. It looked like a lovely place to nap.

No hammering. No sawing. No sweeping or mopping or dusting. No rattling chairs and clattering tables. No hooting owls.

Finally, Beauty would get some sleep!

5

Beauty stared at the ceiling. A crack ran across it. It looked like a crown.

She rolled over. Now the crack looked like a pointy collar.

She stood up. She turned around twice in a circle. She lay back down.

Something was wrong. Beauty the sleepy kitten wasn't sleepy at all!

Her mind was whirling. It wouldn't let

her sleep. She had never had so much to think about before!

First she thought about the star shower. She couldn't wait to see it.

Then she thought about the party. Just what kind of puppet show would there be? Maybe it would have animal puppets. Maybe it would have a cat puppet!

She thought about the woods. They weren't scary at all. It was silly of her to have been so afraid of them.

Beauty thought about her new animal friends—birds, squirrels, chipmunks, and bunnies. And the owl, of course.

She thought about Aurora. What was it like to grow up in this cottage? What had Aurora been like before she knew she was a princess? Beauty bet that she was every bit as sweet as she was now.

Normally, Beauty didn't have anything very important to think about. She thought about her ribbons and bows. She thought about getting her fur brushed. She thought about

caviar. She thought about napping.

But so much had happened today! She didn't really want to fall asleep. What if there was more to see?

She heard whispers from downstairs. She heard soft laughter and singing. The other animals were being quiet—just for her.

But what were they talking about now?

Beauty heard Bloom laugh. What was the joke? Who had told it?

Beauty felt left out.

She leaped from the bed. She tiptoed down the stairs. She peeked around the tree trunk at the bottom of the stairs.

The animals were gathered in a circle on the rug. Bloom was telling a story. She was whispering. Beauty couldn't hear her. She snuck in closer.

"And then Aurora said to Prince Phil—" Bloom caught sight of Beauty and stopped. "Oh, Beauty! I'm sorry! Did we wake you? Were we too loud?"

Beauty shook her head. "No," she said. "I was too excited to sleep. I wanted to see what you all were doing."

Bloom laughed. "You? Couldn't sleep? This must be the first time ever."

Beauty's pink nose turned even pinker. "I know!"

"Some things are better than sleeping," one of the squirrels said. "Like hanging out with friends."

"I'm glad you're awake," Bloom said. "It's more fun with you here. Want to see my star dance?"

Beauty nodded.

Beauty and Bloom and their new friends sat around talking and laughing and telling stories. Bloom performed her star dance. It was lovely! She leaped and cantered like she was riding a shooting

star. Beauty was so proud of her friend.

They drank cool water pulled from the stream. They ate nuts and berries. It wasn't caviar, but it was very tasty. The floor was hard, not like Beauty's plush pillows. But Beauty didn't mind.

Outside the cottage, the sun set. The sky got dark. The stars came out.

Inside the cottage, no one noticed. Beauty didn't fall asleep once, not even for a minute.

Suddenly, the door to the cottage creaked open. All the animals turned to see who had opened it. Princess Aurora stepped through the door. She looked around.

"Beauty, there you are!" she cried. She rushed over to where the animals were sitting. "I've been looking all over for you!"

The star shower! Aurora's party!

Beauty had forgotten about them. She had promised to be there. Had she missed the whole thing?

Aurora swept Beauty into her arms. She nuzzled the back of her ears.

"Don't worry," she said. "It's not midnight yet. I was getting ready, but I couldn't find you or Bloom anywhere.

Merryweather told me where to go."

She looked around the cottage. "You found my old home! And my wonderful old friends." The animals gathered around Aurora. She greeted them one by one.

"Everyone should come to my party," she said. "But we have to hurry!"

The chipmunks put away the nuts and berries. The bunnies swept the floor with their cottontails. The birds pulled the curtains shut. Then Aurora and all her friends left the cottage. They hurried through the woods. They made it to the castle just before midnight.

The castle was lit up as if stars had already fallen onto its stone walls. Torches lined the walkways. Lanterns lit the halls. In the courtyard, the puppet show was under way.

Beauty craned her head as she passed. There was a cat puppet!

"We can come back later," Aurora told her. "The puppet show will be here for a week."

They went to the middle of the garden. Soft pillows were piled on the grass. Aurora sat on one. Beauty sat next to her. Bloom sat on the other side. They turned their faces to the sky just as the stars began to drop.

Beauty was wide awake. She didn't even blink. The star shower was the most beautiful thing she had ever seen. It was like good fairy magic raining through a midnight-blue sky.

"That was amazing," Bloom said as the star shower began to slow down.

Beauty smiled. "It was definitely worth staying awake for," she said.

Then, with a little bow to Aurora, Bloom began her star dance. Aurora clapped and swayed along with the beat.

Beauty had never felt so happy. She had learned so much today!

She learned that she was braver than she thought. She learned that the woods weren't so spooky. She learned that some things were more fun than sleeping.

"I have another surprise," Aurora said. She touched Beauty on the tip of her nose. "Come with me!"

Another surprise? Beauty doubted that this day could get any better.

Beauty followed Aurora to a terrace that overlooked the palace garden. She gasped when she saw what was there—

A new kitten bed!

It wasn't just any kitten bed, though. It was a big, fancy lounge chair. It had lots of fluffy, colorful pillows piled on top. They looked as soft as clouds.

Beauty climbed on top of the pillows. She kneaded them with her paws. She turned around twice. She lay down. Then she purred. It was perfect.

Seconds later, Beauty fell asleep.

Each Palace Pet has a story

to tell–collect them all!

Belle

Teacup

Tiana

Bayou

Ariel

Treasure